What the Ladybird Heard at CHRISTMAS

JULIA DONALDSON

LYDIA MONKS

On Christmas Eve when the sun was low
And the fields and woods were white with snow,
The ladybird set off to spend
A couple of nights with a spider friend.

The spider lived in a big old house
With people and pets and a small white mouse.

And the small white mouse said,
"Squeak, squeak, squeak!"

And the hamster's wheel went
Creak, creak, creak.

The parrot squawked,
the canary sang,

And the spider twanged her web
— twang, twang!

The Great Dane snored and the Siamese purred,
But the ladybird said never a word.

But the ladybird saw,
and the ladybird heard . . .

She saw two men with a big black van,
A ladder, a sack and a cunning plan.
(The ladybird already knew
They were Lanky Len and Hefty Hugh.)
And she heard Hugh whisper, "Listen, Len –
We'll wait until it's night, and then
When Santa Claus has been and gone
We'll put our fancy costumes on.

You'll look lovely as an elf,
And I'll be Santa Claus himself.
We'll climb to the chimney, then down we'll slide,
And before we know it, we'll be inside!"

Said Len, "They say that house is haunted
But we're both brave — we won't be daunted.
Later on those girls and boys
Will have their stockings filled with toys!
We'll take those stockings off their beds.
They won't wake up, the sleepy heads.
And even if they do awake,
They'll think we've come to give, not take!"

The two thieves chuckled, "Ha, ha, ha!
What clever, crafty chaps we are!"

Then the little spotty ladybird
Who hardly ever spoke a word
Told the others what she'd heard . . .

And the mouse said, "Squeak!" and the wheel went creak,
And both the birds gave a piercing shriek.
The spider scuttled, the Great Dane growled,
And the Siamese arched her back and yowled,
And all of the pets said, "How unpleasant!
We can't let them steal one single present!"

But the ladybird had a good idea
And she whispered it into each animal ear.

Then they found a sheet of the perfect size
And the parrot pecked two holes for eyes.
The spider spun, and the Siamese cat
Slunk out to chat to a friendly bat.

Upstairs, the children — Flo, Fleur, Fred
And little Finn — were snug in bed.
Then Santa came with treats and toys
For all four lucky girls and boys.

The thieves kept watch until he'd gone,
Then they put their fancy costumes on.

They climbed to the chimney and down they slid.
"They're here!" hissed the cat, and the pets all hid.

The small white mouse was ready. Hop!
She leapt and she crept inside Len's top,
And Lanky Len began to whine,
"There's fingers crawling up my spine!"

The hamster's wheel creaked round and round,
And Hugh said, "That's an eerie sound!"

The spider wound her silky threads
All around the robbers' heads,

And Len said, "This is awfully rummy."
"I'm scared!" cried Hugh. "I want my mummy!"

The Siamese cat let out a yowl.
"Oh crumbs!" said Len. "A ghostly howl!"

The canary sang, "Beware! Beware!"
As they turned the corner of the stair,

And there they saw a dreadful sight . . .

Something scary, tall and white.

That second, the parrot shouted, "Boo!"
"HELP! A GHOST!" yelled Len and Hugh.

They fell downstairs and they charged outside,
But who was waiting?

"Bats!" they cried.

And frightened for their lives they ran
All the way back to their big black van.
The bats flapped after the two bad men,
And they never went back to that house again.

Then the small white mouse said, "Squeak, squeak, squeak!"
And the hamster's wheel went Creak, creak, creak.
The parrot squawked, the canary sang
And the spider twanged her web — twang, twang!
The Great Dane woofed and the Siamese purred,

But the ladybird said never a word.

For Adalyn ~ JD
For Miles and Florrie ~ LM

First published 2022 by Macmillan Children's Books
This edition published 2023 by Macmillan Children's Books
an imprint of Pan Macmillan
The Smithson, 6 Briset Street, London EC1M 5NR
EU representative: Macmillan Publishers Ireland Limited,
1st Floor, The Liffey Trust Centre,
117-126 Sheriff Street Upper, Dublin 1, D01 YC43

Associated companies throughout the world.
www.panmacmillan.com

ISBN: 978-1-5290-8708-6
Text copyright © Julia Donaldson 2022
Illustrations copyright © Lydia Monks 2022

1 3 5 7 9 8 6 4 2

A CIP catalogue record for this book is available from the British Library.

Printed in China.

Pan Macmillan does not have any control over, or any responsibility for,
any author or third party websites referred to in or on this book.

Image of Anne Boleyn used in collage © Shawshots / Alamy Stock Photo 2022

FSC
www.fsc.org
MIX
Paper | Supporting
responsible forestry
FSC® C116313